The Fetch

Brandon Robshaw

Published in association with
The Basic Skills Agency

Hodder & Stoughton

A MEMBER OF THE HODDER HEADLINE GROUP

Acknowledgements
Cover: Dave Smith
Illustrations: Maureen Carter

Orders: please contact Bookpoint Ltd, 39 Milton Park, Abingdon, Oxon OX14
4TD. Telephone: (44) 01235 400414, Fax: (44) 01235 400454. Lines are open
from 9.00–6.00, Monday to Saturday, with a 24 hour message answering service.
Email address: orders@bookpoint.co.uk

British Library Cataloguing in Publication Data
A catalogue record for this title is available from The British Library

ISBN 0 340 74240 2

First published 1999
Impression number   10 9 8 7 6 5 4 3 2
Year   2004 2003 2002 2001 2000

Copyright © 1999 Brandon Robshaw

Typeset by Fakenham Photosetting Ltd, Fakenham, Norfolk.
Printed in Great Britain for Hodder & Stoughton Educational, a division of
Hodder Headline Plc, 338 Euston Road, London NW1 3BH by Athenaeum Press,
Gateshead.

The Fetch

Contents

1	The Stranger	1
2	The Mirror Factory	5
3	The Legend of the Fetch	10
4	Overworking?	14
5	The Doctor	17
6	Some Advice	20
7	Face to Face	23
8	Fetched	26

1

The Stranger

John was scared.

He'd been scared for days now.

Ever since the stranger

had started following him.

The stranger was a tall, thin man –

the same build as John.

He always wore a black hat

and a black coat

with the collar turned up.

John had never seen his face.

He had no idea why

the stranger was following him.

Every time he went out,

the stranger was there,

quietly walking behind him.

Not too close –

about 50 paces behind.

Sometimes John felt like

going up to the man

and asking him what he was playing at.

But he didn't have the nerve.

There was something odd about the man –

something that gave John the creeps.

It got so

that John didn't want to leave the house.

When the weekend came,

he stayed indoors.

But he had to go out again
on Monday morning
to go to work.

He had his breakfast
and put his coat on.
He opened the front door
and looked up and down the street.
It was a grey, winter morning.
There was no sign of the stranger.
John gave a sigh of relief.
He set off.

He looked round at the end of the road.
A chill ran through him.
There was the stranger again,
walking along behind him, with his head down.
He was closer to John now –
only about 40 paces behind.

2

The Mirror Factory

John walked to the station

as quickly as he could.

He didn't look behind him again.

The train pulled into the station.

Out of the corner of his eye

John thought he saw

the stranger getting into the next carriage.

But he couldn't be sure.

When he got off the train,
John ran through the ticket barrier
and hurried to work without looking back.
For once, he was glad to get to work.

John worked in a mirror factory.

It was his job to cut the glass

into different shapes and sizes

to be made into mirrors.

It was very busy that morning

and, what with all the work he had on,

John forgot about the stranger for a while.

The roar of the cutting machine

filled his ears.

He had to keep his mind on his work,

or he could lose a finger.

The morning went by quickly.

At lunch time,

John sat in the canteen

with his friends Sam and Morag.

He'd ordered pie, chips and beans.

He felt relaxed now.

He'd forgotten all about the stranger.

Then John happened to look up.

He saw the stranger

in his black hat and black coat

on the other side of the canteen.

He was standing in the queue,

with a tray in his hand.

John dropped his knife and fork with a clatter.

'What's the matter?' asked Morag.

'You look as if you've seen a ghost,' said Sam.

'He's followed me here!' said John.

'Who?'

'The man in black!' said John.

'He's there! Look!'

Morag looked round.

'I can't see a man in black,' she said.

'There's no one there,' said Sam.

It was true.

There was no one there.

The man in black had gone,

as suddenly and silently as he had arrived.

But John knew he'd be back.

John was right.

That night,

as he walked home from the station,

he glanced behind him.

It was a dark, foggy evening

and he could only see about 30 paces.

But that was far enough to see

the tall, thin figure following him.

3

The Legend of the Fetch

All through the week,

the stranger followed John

more and more closely.

By Friday, he was only about 15 paces behind.

The strange thing was that

John couldn't hear the man's footsteps at all.

He trod as silently as a cat.

Perhaps he was wearing trainers.

John knew he should turn round

and face the man,

but he didn't dare.

He still hadn't seen the man's face properly.

He wasn't sure that he wanted to.

On Friday evening, after work,

John went out for a drink

with Sam and Morag.

They always did this on Fridays.

'You look a bit worried, John,' said Morag.

'To tell you the truth, I am,' said John.

'I think I'm being followed.'

'Who by?' asked Sam.

'Some bloke in a black hat and coat.'

'The one you thought you saw

in the canteen the other day?' asked Morag.

She sounded very interested in John's story.

'That's the one. I don't know why
I keep seeing him but –
Oh, no!' said John.
He had seen the stranger standing by the bar
with his hat tipped over his eyes.
He pointed with a trembling finger.
'There he is! Can't you see him?'
Sam and Morag both looked round.
But the stranger had vanished.

'He was there just now,' said John.
'A tall, thin man – about my size.
He gives me the creeps, I can tell you.'

'About your size?' asked Morag.
'Have you seen his face?'
She sounded even more interested.
She was Scottish and liked tales of ghosts
and strange happenings.

'No, I haven't seen his face.'

'I hope it's not your Fetch!' said Morag.

'My Fetch?' asked John. 'What's that?'

'We've a legend back in Scotland,'
said Morag, 'that when it's time for you
to die, a stranger will come to fetch you
to the land of death. That's why
he's called a Fetch, you understand.
But when you come to look in
the face of that stranger,
it's no stranger – '
(Morag lowered her voice)
' – it's your own self!'

4

Overworking?

Sam looked at John's terrified face
and laughed.
'Don't take any notice of Morag!' he said.
'She's winding you up –
trying to scare you.
There's no such thing as a Fetch.'

'Why do I keep seeing this stranger, then?'
asked John.

'I reckon you're just imagining it,'
said Sam. 'You've been working too hard.
The mind plays strange tricks
when you're tired.'

'I hope you're right,' said John.
'Course I'm right,' said Sam.
'You should go and see a doctor about it.
You might get a few days off work!'

When John left the pub,
he walked home
through the chilly winter night
without looking behind him.
He didn't want to risk seeing
the stranger again.
But all the way home, he had a sense that
there was someone close behind.

When he got in,

he looked out of the window.

The stranger was there in the street,

walking to and fro outside the house,

lit up in the yellow glare of a street lamp.

5

The Doctor

John thought about Sam's advice

all through the next day.

He didn't really like going to doctors.

He didn't want to be told he was going mad.

On the other hand,

he couldn't stand seeing that stranger

everywhere he went.

Maybe the doctor could help.

John made up his mind
just as night was falling.
He'd go and see the doctor.
But he didn't walk there.
He didn't want to be followed again.
He took a taxi.

The doctor's surgery felt warm and safe.
There was nowhere for the stranger
to hide in here, thought John.

'What seems to be the trouble?'
asked the doctor.

'I think I'm being followed,' said John.
'Either that or I'm seeing things.'
He told the doctor all about the tall,
thin stranger in the black coat and hat.

'Interesting,' said the doctor.

'What do you think might be causing this?'

'One of my friends thinks it's a Fetch.

A Fetch is a stranger who comes

to fetch you to the land of death.

Only when you look in their face,

it's not a stranger.

It's your double.

Your own self.'

The doctor raised her eyebrows.

'But another friend thinks

I'm just seeing things,' said John.

'He thinks I've been overworking.

What do you think, doctor?'

6

Some Advice

'I think you've been overworking,'
said the doctor.
'Where do you work?'
'In a mirror factory.'
'Ah,' said the doctor.
'That might explain it.
You see yourself in mirrors
all day at work, I suppose.'
'Well, yes.'

'So it's not surprising that your fantasy

should take this form –

a stranger who is really you.

That's what you see at work all day long!'

'A fantasy?' said John.

'You mean there is no stranger?'

'I'd say there are lots of strangers.

Every time you see someone in a coat and hat,

you think it's the same person.

After all, it's not unusual

to wear a hat and coat at this time of year.

They're all just ordinary people.

No one is following you.'

John thought about this.

'So – what should I do, then?'

'Next time you think you see this stranger,
go up to him. Ask him the time.
You'll soon find out it's just
an ordinary person.'

'Well ... OK,' said John.
He didn't fancy it much.
But he supposed the doctor knew best.
He got up and put his hat on.
He left the safe, warm doctor's surgery
and went out into the cold winter night.

7

Face to Face

Rain fell from the dark sky.

Puddles gleamed yellow

in the light of the street lamps.

A cold wind blew.

John turned up his coat collar.

He tramped briskly down the street.

He wanted to get home

as quickly as possible.

He thought about the doctor's advice.

If the stranger was behind him,

he could turn and face him now.

Ask him the time.

Get it over with.

And the stranger would turn out to be

an ordinary person.

That would be a relief.

Only John didn't want to turn round.

He just kept walking.

The thought that the stranger

might be behind him

made his back tingle.

Don't be a coward, he told himself.

Do it now.

Stop. Turn round.

He stopped.

He turned round.

The stranger was only ten paces behind,

walking silently towards him.

8

Fetched

John's heart beat like a machine-gun.

But he stood his ground.

The stranger walked right up to him
and stopped.

'Excuse me,' said John.

His voice sounded small and far away
in his own ears.

'Excuse me, have you got the time?'

The stranger tilted back his hat.
In the yellow glare of the street lamp,
John saw his own face
staring at him.

John was too terrified to scream.

'The time?' said the Fetch,
and the voice was John's own.
'It's time to come with me.'

He took John by the arm
and led him away down the street.

They turned the corner
and were lost from sight.

The yellow street lamps
shone down on the wet, empty street.